Going by Plane

by Susan Ashley

Reading consultant: Susan Nations, M.Ed., author/literacy coach/consultant

Please visit our web site at: **www.earlyliteracy.cc**
For a free color catalog describing **Weekly Reader**® Early Learning Library's
list of high-quality books, call 1-877-445-5824 (USA) or 1-800-387-3178 (Canada).
Weekly Reader® Early Learning Library's fax: (414) 336-0164.

Library of Congress Cataloging-in-Publication Data

Ashley, Susan.
    Going by plane / by Susan Ashley.
      p. cm. — (Going places)
    Includes bibliographical references and index.
    ISBN 0-8368-3731-2 (lib. bdg.)
    ISBN 0-8368-3836-X (softcover)
    1. Aeronautics—Juvenile literature. 2. Air travel—Juvenile literature. [1. Airplanes.
  2. Air travel.] I. Title.
  TL547.A783   2003
  629.13—dc21   2003045037

This edition first published in 2004 by
Weekly Reader® Early Learning Library
330 West Olive Street, Suite 100
Milwaukee, WI 53212 USA

Art direction: Tammy Gruenewald
Photo research: Diane Laska-Swanke
Editorial assistant: Erin Widenski
Cover and layout design: Katherine A. Goedheer

Photo credits: Cover, title, pp. 10, 11, 14, 17, 18, 19 © Gregg Andersen; p. 4 © Library of Congress;
pp. 5, 8 Javier Flores/www.ronkimballstock.com; pp. 6, 7 © Underwood Archives; pp. 9, 15, 21
Katherine A. Goedheer/© Weekly Reader® Early Learning Library, 2004; pp. 12, 13 © Gibson Stock
Photography; p. 16 © Gary J. Benson; p. 20 © Nova Development Corporation

Printed in the United States of America

1 2 3 4 5 6 7 8 9 07 06 05 04 03

Table of Contents

The Wright brothers' plane may look simple to us today, but it changed the history of flying.

Early Planes

On December 17, 1903, two brothers named Wilbur and Orville Wright achieved what no one else had ever been able to do — the world's first successful airplane flight! Their plane became the model for future airplanes.

Airplanes need wings to lift them off the ground and hold them in the air. Many early planes had two sets of wings to give them more lift. These airplanes were called biplanes.

Biplanes have two sets of wings to help lift them off the ground.

People enjoyed watching stunts like this during the 1920s.

In the 1920s, biplanes raced each other and performed stunts in the air in front of amazed crowds. You can still watch biplanes performing stunts at air shows today.

Pilots competed to see who could fly the farthest. In 1927, Charles Lindbergh became the first pilot to fly a plane alone, non-stop, across the Atlantic Ocean.

Charles Lindbergh and his plane, the *Spirit of St. Louis*, made history when they flew non-stop from New York to Paris in 1927.

The DC-3 was the most popular passenger plane in the 1930s.

Passenger Jets

The earliest planes held only one or two people. Passenger planes did not become popular until the 1930s. The first passenger planes had propeller-powered engines. They were not very fast and had to stop often to refuel.

In the 1950s, people began building passenger planes with jet engines. Jet engines allowed planes to fly faster and farther than ever before. More and more people began flying. Today, passenger jets carry people all over the world.

This map shows routes for an airline that is based in Atlanta, Georgia.

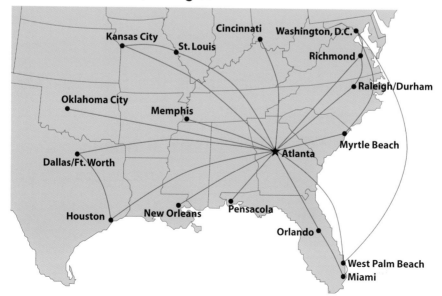

A 747 is easy to recognize because of the large "hump" on top of the plane.

The largest passenger jet is the Boeing 747. It holds more than 400 people and can stay in the air for 17 hours before it has to refuel. A 747's top speed is 604 miles (972 kilometers) per hour — three times faster than the passenger planes of the 1930s.

People traveling on a passenger jet begin their trip at the airport. When they arrive at the airport, they check their luggage and get a boarding pass. All passengers must pass through a security checkpoint. All carry-on items must pass through a scanner.

This passenger has arrived at the airport. He and his luggage will pass a security checkpoint before boarding the plane.

The cockpit of an airplane contains many dials.

Pilots sit in a cockpit at the front of the plane. The cockpit has all of the instruments that pilots need to control the plane. Pilots use radios to talk to air traffic controllers on the ground.

Air traffic controllers control airplane traffic in the air and on the ground. They use radar to keep track of planes in the sky. They tell pilots when it is safe to take off. They make sure the runways are clear for landing.

Air traffic controllers control the flow of airplane traffic in and out of the airport.

Large planes like the 747 reach high speeds at takeoff.

Airplanes take off on a runway. Airplanes use the runway to build up speed. The bigger and heavier the plane, the more speed it needs to get off the ground. A heavy plane like the 747 goes 180 miles (290 km) per hour at takeoff.

The Concorde is the fastest passenger jet in the world. It has reached speeds of 1,490 miles (2,400 km) per hour. That is faster than the speed of sound! Everything about the Concorde is designed for high speed, including its pointed nose and its swept-back wings.

This graph shows the top speeds of different types of airplanes.

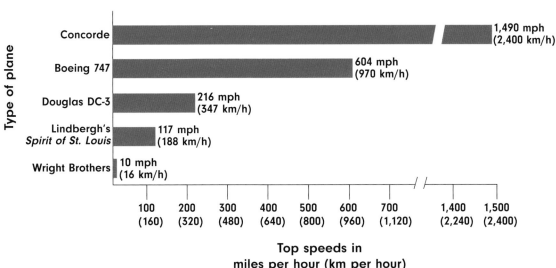

Crop dusters fly close to the ground when they spray crops.

Special Planes

There are many types of planes. Crop dusters are small planes that spray crops. Small planes are used for other jobs as well. They plant seeds and help fight forest fires. Some small planes can even write in the sky!

Seaplanes take off and land on water. They have pontoons instead of wheels, so they can float on water. People use seaplanes to get to islands or lakes where there are no runways. For a seaplane, water is the runway!

This seaplane can land on water because it has pontoons instead of wheels.

Cargo planes unload freight when they arrive at an airport and pick up new freight before they take off again.

Cargo planes carry freight instead of people. They carry everything from small parcels to big machinery. Companies that deliver overnight packages use cargo planes. There are no seats in a cargo plane. The inside of the plane is completely filled with freight.

A helicopter has long, narrow blades instead of wings. When the blades spin, the helicopter lifts straight into the air. Unlike airplanes, helicopters can fly backwards and sideways and hover in the air. They can even land on top of buildings!

The blades on this helicopter lift it into the air. The skids on the bottom of the helicopter are used for landing.

This navy plane is taking off from a ship called an aircraft carrier.

The military has its own planes. Navy planes take off and land on aircraft carriers. Huge cargo planes carry troops, equipment, and food. The stealth bomber looks like a flying triangle. How airplanes have changed since the first flight in 1903!

Time Line of Famous "Firsts"

1903	Wright brothers' first flight
1927	Charles Lindbergh's historic trans-Atlantic flight; *Spirit of St. Louis*
1930s	First passenger planes
1950s	First jet-engine passenger planes
1970	First Boeing 747 goes into service
1976	Concorde begins flying
1988	First stealth bomber is displayed

Glossary

achieve — to reach a goal through hard work or effort

checkpoint — a place where travelers are stopped for inspection

freight — goods carried from one place to another

hover — to hang in the air

instruments — mechanical or electronic devices

pontoons — hollow supports on the bottom of a plane for floating on water

radar — a device used to find the location of an object

scanner — a device that can "see" through baggage to check what is inside

stealth — secret; difficult to see

For More Information

Books

Hunter, Ryan Ann. *Take Off!* New York: Holiday House, 2000.

Maynard, Christopher. *Airplane*. New York: DK Publishing, 1995.

Mellett, Peter. *Flight*. Milwaukee: Gareth Stevens, 1998.

Royston, Angela. *Planes*. New York: Little Simon, 1992.

Web Sites

The Flying Clippers

www.flyingclippers.com/main.html

Photos and history of famous seaplanes

How Things Fly

www.nasm.si.edu/galleries/gal109

An exhibition about flight from the National Air and Space Museum

Wright Brothers Aeroplane Company and Museum of Pioneer Aviation

www.wrightbros.org/

Photos and stories of early aviation

Index